*For Creed and Amzy -- my little pumpkins
and for my mother who taught me
to look to the imperfect to find potential.*

The Perfectly Imperfect PUMPKIN

Written by Christina Cody

Illustrated by Lowell Hildebrandt

AuthorHouse™
1663 Liberty Drive
Bloomington, IN 47403
www.authorhouse.com
Phone: 1-800-839-8640

© 2010 Christina Cody. All rights reserved.

No part of this book may be reproduced, stored in a retrieval system,
or transmitted by any means without the written permission of the author.

First published by AuthorHouse   5/26/2010

ISBN: 978-1-4490-7537-8 (sc)

Library of Congress Control Number: 2010903448

Printed in the United States of America
Bloomington, Indiana

This book is printed on acid-free paper.

The brisk fall breeze tiptoed across Amy's nose and whispered in her ears. She slowly strolled with her mother, lazily eyeing the rows and rows and rows of eager *take me home* pumpkins.

With her hand firmly pressed in her mother's, she asked "Can I really have any one I want?"

"Any one you would like," her mother replied.

Amy eagerly looked around the pumpkin patch. Large ones, small ones, round and oblong ones sat anxiously awaiting her decision.

Like the wind, the pumpkins seemed to be whispering to her:

After watching Amy poke, prod, and listen to the pumpkins' requests, her mother suggested, "Look for the pumpkin that seems lonely among this chorus of take me homes—the one that may not be perfect to anyone but you."

While Amy wandered with a deliberate, slow pace, her eyes carefully stumbled over the perfectly round, perfectly orange squash until they rested upon him—a pumpkin barely able to hold steady his own misshapenness.

Oh how he wanted a home, but he was not like the other pumpkins. He was too shy to whisper to Amy. He leaned ever so slightly to the right, desperately trying to straighten his yellowish-orange, egg-shaped body.

He didn't have to work so hard at being noticed. Amy saw the oddly shaped pumpkin and had already decided he was the one that needed a home.

She skipped to her new friend, dropped to her knees, and began rubbing the dust and dirt from his grooves. He seemed to straighten a little at her touch.

Amy's fingertips traced over the pumpkin where she could already see his triangle shaped eyes and smiling, U-shaped mouth with one dangling tooth.

Looking up at her mother, she whispered, "This is the one I want to take home."

Her mother smiled and said, "I think you have made a wonderful choice," and then she carefully picked up the pumpkin, settled him in the crook of her left arm, and extended her right hand to Amy.

Their fingers found their comfortable, loving embrace,
and the three of them headed to the car.

As they passed the rows and rows of perfect pumpkins, Amy smiled, the wind kissed her cheek, and the misshapen pumpkin blushed the most brilliant shade of orange as he whispered a *thank you* to Amy.